The Berenstain Bears®
LONG, LONG AGO

Long, long ago, in ancient days,
pyramids rose and palaces fell.
Let's venture back into the past—
and to the present time—farewell!

Mike Berenstain

Based on the characters created by
Stan and Jan Berenstain

An Imprint of HarperCollinsPublishers

Brother, Sister, and Honey were playing Buried Treasure.

"Dig here!" said Sister. "We'll soon be rich beyond our wildest dreams."

They dug away.

"Clunk!" went the shovel.

"We found something," said the cubs. "Buried treasure!"

They dug it up. But it turned out to be just an old toy truck.

"Hey!" said Brother, surprised. "This is mine. I lost it a long time ago."

The cubs dug some more.
"Clunk!" went the shovel.
"More treasure!" said Sister.
It turned out to be an old plastic bowl.
"Mama must have lost this on a backyard picnic," said Brother.

They dug some more.
"Clunk!" went the shovel.
It was a rusty old hammer.
"Papa must have dropped it when he was fixing something," said Brother.

The cubs showed their finds to Mama and Papa.

"Very interesting," said Papa. "I was reading in the newspaper that Professor Actual Factual is digging up things from the past near his museum."

The cubs were curious.

"Can we go and see?" they asked.

Mama and Papa were happy to take the cubs to the museum. When they arrived, they saw the professor and his helpers digging in the earth nearby.

"Hello, Bear family!" said the professor. "Have you come to see what we're up to?"

"Yes, Professor," said Mama and explained about the cubs' backyard finds.

"We're doing pretty much the same thing here," said the professor. "But we're digging deeper and finding things that are a bit older. We have a display in the museum to show what life was like in Bear Country when the things we're finding here were brand-new. Come along and I'll show you."

The museum was full of interesting things. There were dinosaur fossils, antique cars, Native Bear totem poles, precious gems and minerals, and cases of brightly colored butterflies. They soon came to the Hall of History.

HALL OF HISTORY

"This display shows what life was like in Bear Country about one hundred years ago."

There were statues of bears in an old-fashioned room. They wore funny old clothes. They sat on funny old furniture. There were old-fashioned phones, record players, and lamps.

"Wouldn't it be fun if we could go back in time and really visit the past?" said Sister.

"Hmm!" said the professor. "I have something that may interest you. Follow me."

Puzzled, the Bear family followed along.

100 YEARS AGO

The professor led them up a spiral staircase to his lab at the top of the museum tower. There he showed them a strange-looking machine.

"What is it?" asked Papa.

"It's my Anytime–Anyyear Machine," he said. "With it, I can travel through time. We can use it to learn about the past."

ANYTIME – ANYYEAR MACHINE

"That's amazing!" said Sister.
"Yes, isn't it?" agreed the professor. "Now come along—all aboard!"
"Is it safe?" asked Mama.
"Perfectly," said the professor. "Hold tight!"

He pulled a lever. The room whirled and swirled. They felt dizzy. When the whirling stopped, they were on the banks of a broad, brown river.

"Welcome to ancient Egypt," said the professor. "We are on the banks of the river Nile in the northeast of Africa. Here, the Egyptians made great buildings and statues of stone. The biggest of all were the pyramids—the tombs of the pharaohs who were kings of Egypt. When they died, their bodies were wrapped in cloth and placed inside the pyramids. The cloth-wrapped bodies are called mummies."

"Creepy!" said Papa.

The professor pulled the lever again. They found themselves on the deck of a sailing ship.

"To the north of Egypt across the sea," said the professor, "lay the land of ancient Greece. The Greeks were great sailors. Their ships, called galleys, were powered by oars as well as sails. Eyes were painted on the ships' prows. Maybe they thought this would help the ship 'see' its way through fog and darkness."

2400 YEARS AGO

Their next hop through time took them to a crowded stadium.

"Greece, Egypt, and many other lands were conquered by Rome," explained the professor. "This city in Italy became the center of a great empire. The Romans were famous soldiers. They loved fighting so much, they made a game of it. Slaves called gladiators were forced to fight to the death before cheering crowds in the Colosseum."

"The Roman Empire lasted a long time," the professor continued. "But it was finally destroyed by the barbarians—warrior tribes from the North. This terrible time has been called the Dark Ages."

1500 YEARS AGO

"Europe was broken up into many small countries," said the professor. "These little kingdoms fought among themselves. Rulers lived in strong castles. Knights in armor rode forth to battle. It was a time of almost constant warfare—the Middle Ages."

"After many years, the learning of ancient times was rediscovered," said the professor. "This time of change was called the Renaissance— a 'rebirth.' The biggest change was in art. Artists began to create paintings that looked like the real world around them."

"Soon, ships sailed across the sea and reached the Americas," the professor went on. "No one in Europe knew about this vast New World. Before long, settlers arrived. Among them were the Pilgrims from England. They called the Native tribes who lived there 'Indians' and needed their help to hunt wild turkey and plant corn. After the first harvest, the Indians joined the Pilgrims in a feast—the very first Thanksgiving."

400 YEARS AGO

"But the settlers of America grew unhappy with England's rule," the professor explained. "They decided to break away and start a new country: the United States of America. A war began between the two sides.

"George Washington was the leader of America's army. They fought against the 'redcoats'—the English soldiers. When the war was won, Washington became the new country's first president."

While the bears watched, redcoats fired their guns and bullets whizzed over their heads.

"We'd better get out of here!" said Papa.

The professor pulled the lever of the time machine and, with a whirl and swirl, they were back in their own time.

"Well," said the professor, "you've learned about the past from ancient times to the birth of our own country—the USA. Does this give you any ideas about digging up things from the past?"

"It sure does!" cried the cubs. "We're going to dig up our whole backyard. Thanks for showing us what it was like long, long ago!"

TODAY!